THE FAIRYTALE HAIRDRESSER

AND RED RIDING HOOD

Abie
Longstaff
&
Lauren
Beard

Smart Cookie

PUFFIN

Kittie Lacey was the best hairdresser in all the land.

Today Fairyland was fizzing with excitement. The Queen of Hearts was holding a baking competition and everyone wanted to win first prize – a golden egg laid by Goose herself.

Kittie had a long list of clients to visit.
She picked up her bicycle from Red's Rides.

"It's so kind of Goose to give away one of her delicious eggs," said Kittie.
"Oh, I hope my granny wins the egg," said Red Riding Hood. "She is famous
throughout Fairyland for her delicious Golden Layer Cake!"

"Granny makes the best cakes," said Mr Wolf. "I wish
I could bake like she does."
"Let's go and see what she's making, Kittie," said Red. "She
might even let us lick the spoon."
"Good idea," said Kittie. "But first I've got to see some clients
who need my help ~ come with me!"

First, they stopped at Rapunzel's castle.

"Thank goodness you're here, Kittie," cried Rapunzel.
"I'm making Forest Fruit Bread for the competition
and I can't remember how to plait it – you
always plait my hair!"

"I can help with that," said Kittie. She showed Rapunzel
how to plait one, two, three – over and over.

Next, they visited the Three Bears.

"We're making Honey Cake!" said Baby Bear proudly.

"I can see!" Kittie giggled. "You've got honey stuck in your fur."
She sprayed Baby Bear with conditioner and combed the honey out
until he was soft and fluffy again.

At last they arrived at Granny's.

Kittie rang the bell. But there was no answer.
"That's strange," she said. "The door is
half open . . ." She pushed it wider.

"Granny?" called Red.

"Something is wrong," said Kittie.
"Granny's table has been knocked over,
and her teacups are on the floor!"

HOME
SWEET
HOME

Outside the cottage, Kittie found a clue. "Look!" she cried. "Wolf prints in the mud!"

"Mr Wolf did sound jealous of Granny's baking," said Red. "He must have kidnapped her!"
"No!" said Kittie. "Mr Wolf is our friend. He would never hurt anyone."
"But he's the only wolf in Fairyland – it's got to be him!" said Red.

Kittie frowned. "Let's follow the trail," she said. "It'll lead us to Granny."
They followed the wolf prints through the woods until they came to . . .

. . . a very peculiar factory!

"Granny!" cried Red. "Oh no! She's all tied up!"
Poor Granny was putting cherries on
a conveyor belt that led to a giant mixer.

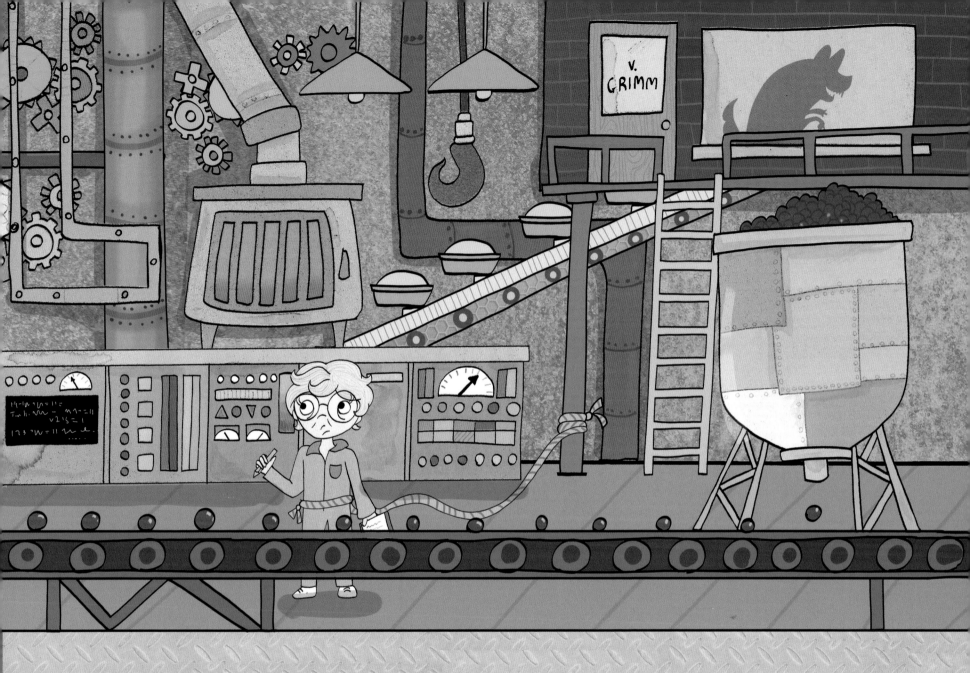

"Red! Kittie!" she sobbed. "Beware of the big bad wolf! He's forcing me
to make my cakes for him so he can win the competition!"
"I knew it!" said Red. "It's Mr Wolf the optician!"
Kittie held her breath.
"Oh dear me, no!" said Granny. "It's another wolf. He's called . . ."

"Von Grimm," growled a voice. "And I won't let
you ruin my secret plan."
Von Grimm snatched Kittie and Red, and tied them up tight!
"I've got it all worked out!" he announced proudly.

He put on a dress. "First, I'm going to pretend to be Granny and win the competition with her cakes."

He put on tights. "Then when I claim my prize, I'll steal the Golden Goose. She will have to lay eggs for me every day. My factory will be the only producer of Golden Layer Cake."

He tied a bonnet on his head. "With Granny's skills plus a lifetime's supply of golden eggs, my cake empire will make millions!"

"You won't get away with this," said Kittie.
"Who's going to stop me?" howled Von Grimm
in triumph. "Not you."
He put Kittie and Red on the conveyor belt and
pulled the lever to turbo speed.
"Any moment now you'll be all mixed up!"

ON

TURBO

Honey

Von Grimm ran out of the factory with a basketful of Granny's cakes.
"Help!" cried Red. She kicked and screamed. Granny burst into tears.
"Don't worry, love," said Kittie. "I know what to do." She wriggled in the ropes
until she could reach her toolbelt . . .

"Hurry!" shouted Red. "We're nearly at the cake mix!"
Kittie's fingers found a scrunchie. Quickly, she tied it
to a ribbon and pinged it as hard as she could.

TWANG!

The scrunchie flew
through the air and
looped round the lever.
Kittie pulled . . .

ON

TURBO

OFF

Honey

. . . until the lever moved to

OFF!

The conveyor belt stopped.

Kittie took out her scissors and cut everyone free.
"Hooray!" cheered Red.
"To the village!" cried Kittie. "We have to stop that wicked wolf."

But the competition was over!
"Congratulations to our winner ~ Granny!"
said the Queen of Hearts.
"Stop!" shouted Kittie. "That isn't Granny ~ look what big ears he has!"
"Oh," gasped the queen.
"Look what big eyes he has!" said Red.
"Ah," cried the crowd.

Von Grimm gave a loud growl . . .

He pulled off his bonnet. "And look what big teeth I have!"

"He's a wolf!" cried Granny. "He kidnapped me and stole my cakes.
And now he's after the Golden Goose!"

"I AM a wolf," growled Von Grimm as he reached for Goose.
"You're coming with me!" he snapped.
"Not so fast," said Kittie. She took Granny's hair rollers from her toolbelt and flung
them to the floor. And as Von Grimm lunged towards Goose . . .

"Ow!" He trod on the rollers.
        "Whoa!" He tripped over and . . .   "Arrgghh!"

CRASH

He hit the pedestal stand. The golden egg was tossed up high and . . .

"Guards!" commanded the Queen of Hearts.
"Take him away!"

The queen turned to the crowd.
"That means," she said, "the REAL winner of the competition is . . . Granny!"
Everyone cheered. Goose clapped her wings.

"Thank you," said Granny. "But I'm
so very tired. And I'm all messy."
"Come to my salon, Granny," said
Kittie. "I'll make you a cup of tea."

Kittie washed Granny's hair until it was sparkly clean. Then she found delicious outfits for Granny and Red to wear.

"Now, let's go and celebrate!" said Kittie.

Goose gave Granny a fresh golden egg and, that very afternoon,
Granny made the most wonderful . . .

"Golden Layer Cake!"
cried Red. "Yippee!"

FISH CAKE

They all had a slice. And Granny saved the largest piece for . . .

Kittie Lacey, the best hairdresser in all the land.
"Hooray for Kittie," cried the Queen of Hearts,
and everyone cheered.